This book belongs to:

· ·

There's much more to explore!
For fun and games about this story,
visit: www.winslowpress.com

For my goddaughter, Terryn—
Always let your butterflies go

The Last Dinosaur Egg

Story and Illustrations by
Andrew Hegeman

One bright summer day, a little iceberg came floating down the river. Long ago, the iceberg had been as big as a mountain. It had traveled far, however, and melted. But what was this? Frozen inside was a large brown egg.

At last, the iceberg and egg came to rest on the sandy shore of a small island.

Under the hot summer
sun, the tiny iceberg
got smaller

and

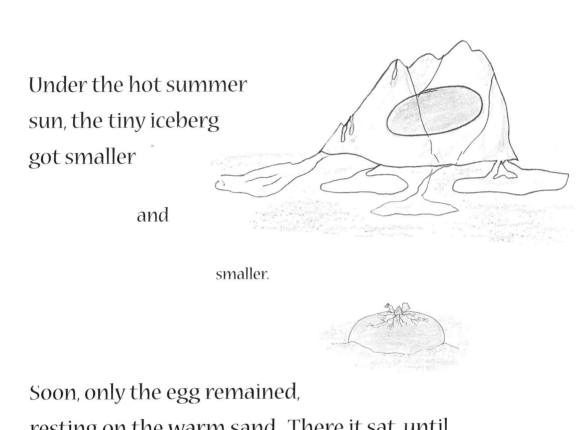

smaller.

Soon, only the egg remained,
resting on the warm sand. There it sat, until
one day large cracks appeared in the shell.
Something was hatching!
What could it be?

It was a baby dinosaur!

Meanwhile, on the other side of the island, Jon and Jenny were chasing butterflies. They often came to the island with their dad, who painted seascapes while they played.

Suddenly, Jon saw a rare purple spotted
butterfly. A chase was on! Jenny and Jon ran
and ran until the tired butterfly landed on
a blue daisy.

Down came Jon's net, catching both the purple spotted butterfly and the surprised baby dinosaur.

Jon and Jenny were surprised too. They let the butterfly go and carefully put the little dinosaur in Jenny's backpack. "Let's not tell anyone about our new pet," Jon said.

And so as Dad drove the boat home, the two children shared a secret smile.

Back home, Jon and Jenny placed the baby dinosaur in an old birdcage that they found in the basement. Then they hid him in their tree house.

Jon scratched his head. "I wonder what kind of dinosaur he is?"

Jenny found a picture in a dinosaur book that looked just like their new pet. "He's a Cory-tho-saurus," she told Jon.

Jon laughed. "That name's too long—let's just call him Cory."

"It says here he's a plant-eater," said Jenny. They tried feeding Cory all sorts of fruits and vegetables, but the little dinosaur wouldn't eat a thing.

Finally, Jenny offered Cory the only vegetable left—a piece of broccoli. Cory's eyes opened wide. Leaping up, he grabbed the broccoli and began to munch and munch and munch.

Every day after that, Jon and Jenny bought more broccoli.

"You two buy broccoli the way most kids buy candy," the grocer chuckled.

Cory ate a **lot** of broccoli. Jon and Jenny had to buy more and more while Cory began to grow

and grow

and grow.

The little dinosaur wasn't so little anymore.

"Look how big Cory is," Jenny said at last. "We've got to get him out of that cage."

But Cory was now too large for the door, so Jon had to use tinsnips to cut him out.

It wasn't long before Cory had grown too big for the tree house. So, one day, using an old sheet and some sturdy rope, they carefully lowered Cory out of the tree house and down to the ground.

Jon and Jenny took Cory inside. When they introduced him to their mom, she shrieked and jumped right out of her sneakers!

Their dad fell over in his chair.

"What do we do now?" Jon asked.

"I know," Jenny said, clapping her hands. "Let's disguise Cory and go to the store for broccoli."

Jenny fetched a big, brown, floppy hat and Mom's old purple coat. Jon found some sunglasses and grabbed the kitchen mop. Then Jon, Jenny, and the disguised dinosaur were off to buy groceries.

Soon they were pushing a cart down the vegetable aisle. "This is working perfectly," Jenny whispered.

All of a sudden, Cory stopped and stared down the aisle. The not-so-little dinosaur started running. Off flew the disguise!

Customers screamed and ran from the store.

What on earth did Cory see?

Broccoli! Cory had never seen so much broccoli.
He snatched up a bunch and began

to munch

and munch

and munch.

The grocer called the police. "There's a monster tearing up my store!" he shouted into the phone.

"We'll be right there," said the chief.

Soon, not only the police, but the army and air force surrounded the supermarket. TV news people arrived and a large crowd began to gather.

Jon and Jenny brought Cory out.
"Don't shoot!" shouted Jon.
"This is our pet dinosaur, Cory.
We'll pay for all the broccoli he ate."
The police chief could see that Cory was
indeed friendly. He knew just what to do.

The chief called the city zoo, which sent over a
big truck. "Don't worry," he told Jon and Jenny.
"Cory will get a swell home and as much broccoli
as he wants. You two can visit any time you like."

That night, Cory's adventure at the supermarket was on the news all over the world. People everywhere were shocked to see a real live dinosaur.

Cory was even given his own island at the zoo, where the lovable dinosaur was very popular. Jon and Jenny were given green zoo caps and made official dinosaur keepers. Every day after school they visited their friend and gave him all the broccoli he wanted.